Postcards from Beth

Written by
Jill Atkins

Illustrated by
Ariane Hofmann-Maniyar

Beth went to the seaside
and she sent some postcards
to her gran.

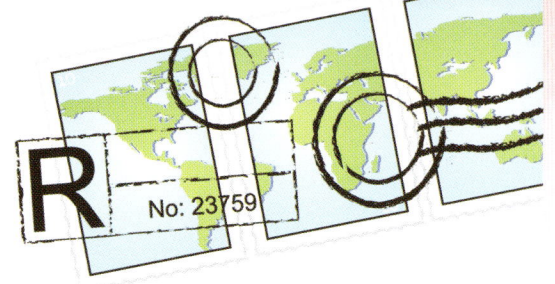

To: Gran

Dear Gran

Today we went to the seaside. I got lots of shells and stones. Then we played in the sea.

Love from Beth

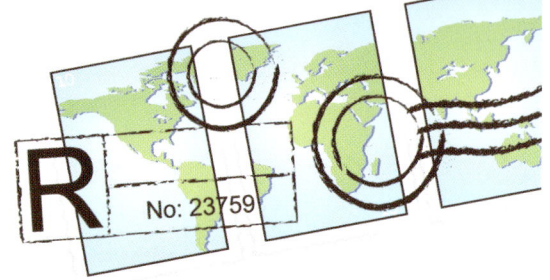

To: Gran

Dear Gran

I made a big sandcastle and I put shells and stones on it.
It was the best sandcastle!

Lots of love
Beth xxx

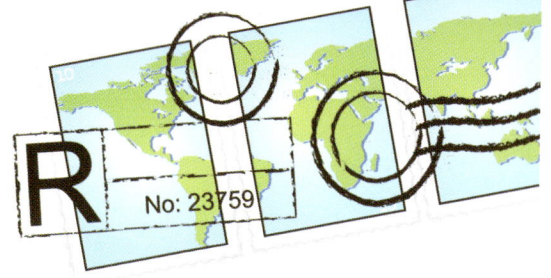

To: Gran

Dear Gran

Today I looked in the rock pools.
I saw some little fish
and I put them in a bucket.

Big hugs
from Beth

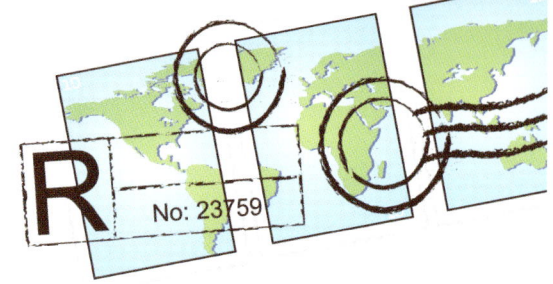

To: Gran

Dear Gran

We had a lot of fun on the sand.
We played football and I got five goals.
I was very happy.

A big hug
from Beth

xxxx

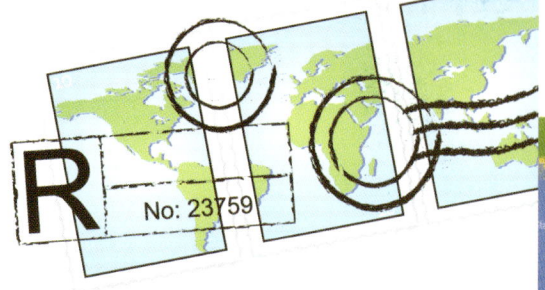

To: Gran

Dear Gran

Today we went in a boat on the sea.
We saw five dolphins.
I love dolphins.

Lots of hugs
Beth

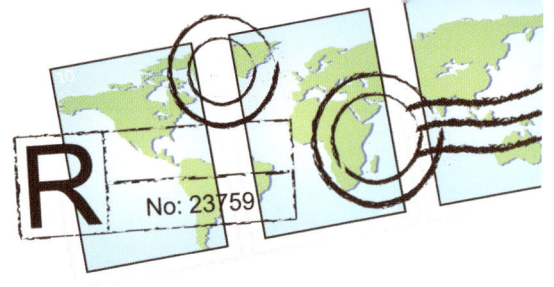

To: Gran

Dear Gran

I took my kite to the seaside.
It went up, up, up into the sky.
It looked very small up there.

Love from
Beth

To: Gran

Dear Gran

Today we have to go home.

Lots of love from
Beth